Simon Can't Say Hippopotamus

by Bonnie Highsmith Taylor

Illustrated by Phyllis Hornung

MONDO

Text copyright © 2003 by Bonnie Highsmith Taylor   Illustrations copyright © 2003 by Phyllis Hornung

under exclusive license to MONDO Publishing

For information contact:

MONDO Publishing

980 Avenue of the Americas

New York, NY 10018

Visit our web site at http://www.mondopub.com

Printed in Canada

Printed in the United States of America

03 04 05 06 07 08 09 HC 9 8 7 6 5 4 3 2 1

03 04 05 06 07 08 09 PB 9 8 7 6 5 4 3 2 1

Designed by Charlie Hunt   ISBN 1-59336-017-7 (hardcover) 1-59336-018-5 (pbk)

Library of Congress Cataloging-in-Publication Data

Taylor, Bonnie Highsmith

Simon can't say hippopotamus / by Bonnie Highsmith Taylor ; illustrated by Phyllis Hornung

p. cm

Summary: Simon's younger sister is so proud of all the things he can do that she does not understand why people get so upset just because he cannot say one word

ISBN 1-59336-017-7 (hc)

ISBN 1-59336-018-5 (pbk)

[1 Brothers and sisters--Fiction

2 Stories in rhyme]

I. Hornung, Phyllis, ill II. Title

PZ8.3 T2145Si 2003

[E]--dc21

2003044912

But Simon can't say hippopotamus,
so people make fun.

4

They laugh and say, "Simon, please try."

"I do. I try,"
is Simon's reply.

And he really does.
So why laugh? Why?

He can make a kite
with paper and string.

With rope and a tire,
he can make a swing.

6

He can count to 100,
make up his bed,
tie his own shoes,

and stand on his head.

But he can't say hippopotamus, so people say, "Oh, my!
I just know you can say it.
You can if you try."

"Now, Simon," says Mother,
"say hip-po real slow."

"Pot-a-mus," says Fathe
"You can do it, I know."

8

"Oh, golly!" cries Simon.
"It just isn't fair."

"I try and I try,
but I can't
—so there!"

9

Simon does lots of things, so he's got to be smart.
With a box and two wheels, he can make a go-cart.

With a box and four wheels, he can make a bus.

But—he just can't say hippopotamus.

10

He can whistle
and yodel
and play a bassoon.

He can tap dance
and tumble
and make up a tune.

11

He can do lots more than I can do.

I can't make my bed or tie my shoe,
or tap dance or yodel or play a bassoon.
I can't even whistle or carry a tune.

12

So why do people make such a fuss
when he can't say hippopotamus?
Why should it worry his father and mother?
It isn't important one way or another.

You'd think they'd be happy and filled with delight to have such a boy. He's so terribly bright!

A boy who's so bright should be just a delight.

14

Once Simon and I went to visit a zoo.
We saw an aardvark and a big kangaroo,
a monkey, a tiger, a bear, a gnu,
a baby armadillo and a hippopotamus, too.

Simon knew the name of each animal there,
Well, I didn't know them—but I didn't care.

He said, "There's an aardvark. They're very rare.
And there's an old grumbly grizzly bear.

That's an armadillo.
His shell's superstrong!"

Then he said, "HIPPOPOTAMUS"—
but it came out all wrong.

It just didn't matter. I didn't mind.
I wouldn't laugh. That wouldn't be kind.

18

For Simon's my friend,
and I wouldn't fuss
just because he can't say
hippopotamus.

19

He can comb his hair, peel a pear,
bake a pie, tie a tie,
land a trout without a doubt,
but that great big word will not come out.

So people worry and people fret.
But Simon is smart. He'll say it yet.

He'll say it some day. Just give him time.
I know he'll do it. He'll do it fine.

Why should it bother his father and mother,

his grandma and grandpa,

his sister and brother?

Why should it bother his uncle and aunt?

It's not that important.
If he can't, he can't.

So let them grumble and mumble and sigh . . .

23

Simon can't say hippopotamus—

and neither can I.